TEN

LITTLE TEDDY BEARS

G000280657

PUFFIN BOOKS

Published by the Penguin Group
Penguin Books Ltd, 27 Wrights Lane, London W8 5TZ, England
Penguin Putnam Inc., 375 Hudson Street, New York, New York 10014, USA
Penguin Books Australia Ltd, Ringwood, Victoria, Australia
Penguin Books Canada Ltd, 10 Alcorn Avenue, Toronto, Ontario, Canada M4V 3B2
Penguin Books (NZ) Ltd, Private Bag 102902, NSMC, Auckland, New Zealand

Penguin Books Ltd, Registered Offices: Harmondsworth, Middlesex, England

First published by Reinhardt Books in association with Viking 1993
Published in Puffin Books 1995
3 5 7 9 10 8 6 4

Copyright © Maureen Roffey, 1993
All rights reserved

The moral right of the author/illustrator has been asserted

Made and printed Italy by Printer Trento Srl

TEN

LITTLE TEDDY BEARS

Maureen Roffey

PUFFIN BOOKS

With Reinhardt Books

Ten little Teddy Bears
sitting down to dine,

One didn't like the soup
and then there were nine.

5

Nine little Teddy Bears
climbing through a gate,

6

One Bear was far too fat
and then there were eight.

7

Eight little Teddy Bears
setting off for Devon,

One Teddy missed the train
and then there were seven.

9

Seven little Teddy Bears
stacking up their bricks,

One built hers much too high
and then there were six.

Six little Teddy Bears
playing round the hive,

12

One Bear was chased away
and then there were five.

Five little Teddy Bears
shopping in a store,

One Bear forgot his purse
and then there were four.

15

Four little Teddy Bears
playing in a tree,

One let go of the branch
and then there were three.

Three little Teddy Bears
visiting the zoo,

One stayed to have a swim
and then there were two.

Two little Teddy Bears
going for a run,

One stopped to buy an ice
and then there was one.

21

One little Teddy Bear
sitting all alone,

Thought a picnic might be fun
so picked up the phone . . .